HOW TO CATCH A RAINBOW

Naomi jones   aNA Gómez

OXFORD
UNIVERSITY PRESS

Freya loved rainbows.

They were full of beautiful colours,
which always made her smile.

She wished, more than anything,
that she had one of her very own.

So she decided to become . . .

. . . a Rainbow Hunter!
Now, all she had to do was find one.

So Freya hunted high and low.

She searched far

and wide.

But there weren't any rainbows anywhere.

Freya was starting to feel a bit fed up,
until she remembered something . . .

. . . rainbows are made from rain and sun.

Rain + Sun = Rainbow!

She decided she would make one.

WATERING CAN

LIGHT (SUN)

WATER (RAIN)

But it didn't work and now she had wet feet!

Freya was disappointed,
but she wasn't going to give up.

There *must* be another way to make a rainbow.

She opened her bag to look for ideas
and suddenly it came to her . . .

. . . she could hunt one colour at a time!

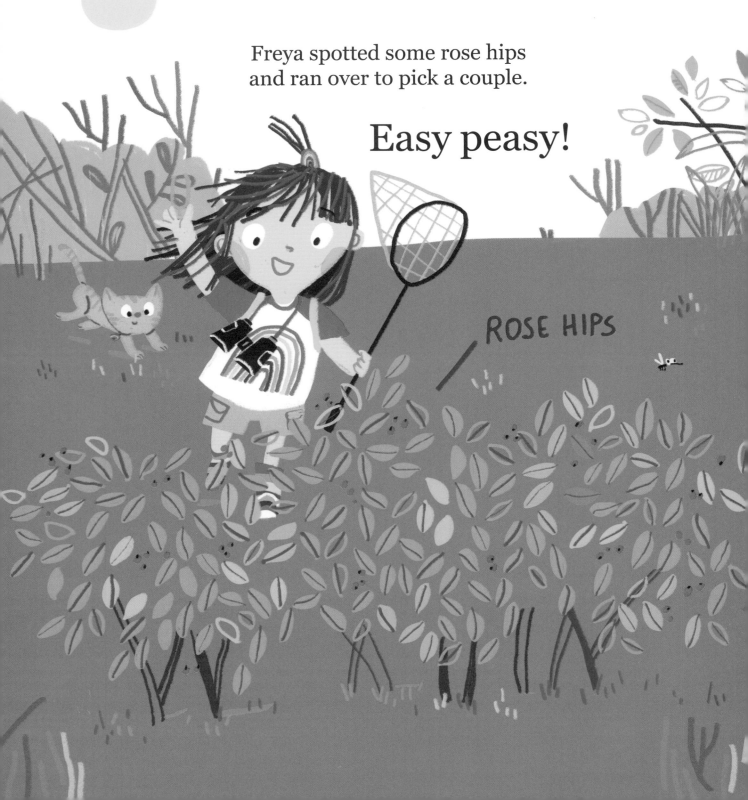

Red was first.

Freya spotted some rose hips
and ran over to pick a couple.

Easy peasy!

ROSE HIPS

But orange was tricky.

None of the leaves had turned orange yet
and all the flowers were other colours.

Freya searched everywhere, until . . .

. . . she spotted a beautiful orange feather!

Yellow was next.

FEATHER

There was the sun, but it was too far away.

So Freya looked around until she found . . .

...an enormous yellow sunflower.

SUNFLOWER

Green was easy too.

She was really getting the hang of this rainbow hunting!

GRASS

Next was blue.

The sky was blue, but that wouldn't do.

So Freya hunted amongst the plants,
and she searched under her toys.

But she still couldn't find anything blue.

It was hopeless.

Freya only had half a rainbow.

What was the point of being a Rainbow Hunter
if she couldn't find all the colours?

Freya threw her bag onto the grass,

stamped her feet,

and flung herself to the ground.

After a few minutes,
she closed her eyes.

Freya took some deep breaths.

She listened to the birds singing
in the trees and it gave her an idea.

Freya leapt up and started climbing
the tallest tree in the garden.

She looked down.
Nothing.
She looked up.
Still nothing.
And then she spotted an old bird's nest.

In it lay a small, cracked . . .

There were just two colours left now.

Indigo was easy.

BLACKBERRIES

And so was violet.

LAVENDER

The Rainbow Hunter had done it!

Freya skipped into the kitchen trailing mud
and victory in her wake.

She emptied her bag and spread all of
her rainbow colours out onto the table.

But something wasn't right . . .

The flowers and leaf were flat, the blackberries were squished and the eggshell was smashed. Even the feather was crumpled.

It was the worst rainbow ever.

LAVENDER

SUNFLOWER

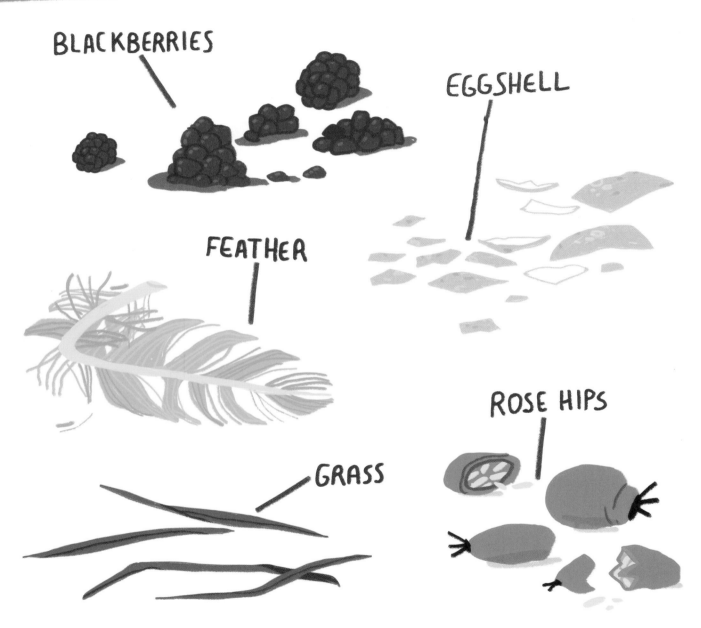

BLACKBERRIES

EGGSHELL

FEATHER

ROSE HIPS

GRASS

Freya didn't know what to do, until Dad pointed out of the window . . .

IT WAS

PERFECT!

'I wish rainbows lasted forever,' said Freya.
'Me too,' agreed Dad.

Freya looked over at all the sad, broken things
on the table and realised something . . .

. . . real rainbows can't be caught or made.

But luckily, Freya had another idea.

She picked up her bag and began a new hunt, for crayons this time.

'Look Dad!' said Freya.
'Now we'll never forget that
rainbow we saw together!'

'It's perfect,' replied Dad.

We've counted over 100 rainbows in this story.
How many can you find?

FOR MY SISTER BETH, WHO ALWAYS BRINGS THE SUNSHINE — NAOMI JONES

FOR MY RAINBOW LOVER, SERGIO — GOMEZ

OXFORD
UNIVERSITY PRESS

Oxford is a registered trademark
of Oxford University Press in the UK
and certain other countries

Words © Naomi Jones 2022
Illustrations © Ana Gomez 2022

First published 2022

This edition published exclusively for
Scottish BookTrust in 2022

British Library Cataloguing
in Publication Data

Data available

ISBN: 978-0-19-278709-5

10 9 8 7 6 5 4 3 2 1

Printed in China

www.oup.com